# Dear Parents:

Congratulations! Your child is taking the first steps on an exciting journey. The destination? Independent reading!

**STEP INTO READING®** will help your child get there. The program offers five steps to reading success. Each step includes fun stories and colorful art or photographs. In addition to original fiction and books with favorite characters, there are Step into Reading Non-Fiction Readers, Phonics Readers and Boxed Sets, Sticker Readers, and Comic Readers—a complete literacy program with something to interest every child.

## Learning to Read, Step by Step!

**Ready to Read    Preschool–Kindergarten**
• big type and easy words • rhyme and rhythm • picture clues
For children who know the alphabet and are eager to begin reading.

**Reading with Help    Preschool–Grade 1**
• basic vocabulary • short sentences • simple stories
For children who recognize familiar words and sound out new words with help.

**Reading on Your Own    Grades 1–3**
• engaging characters • easy-to-follow plots • popular topics
For children who are ready to read on their own.

**Reading Paragraphs    Grades 2–3**
• challenging vocabulary • short paragraphs • exciting stories
For newly independent readers who read simple sentences with confidence.

**Ready for Chapters    Grades 2–4**
• chapters • longer paragraphs • full-color art
For children who want to take the plunge into chapter books but still like colorful pictures.

**STEP INTO READING®** is designed to give every child a successful reading experience. The grade levels are only guides; children will progress through the steps at their own speed, developing confidence in their reading. The F&P Text Level on the back cover serves as another tool to help you choose the right book for your child.

Remember, a lifetime love of reading starts with a single step!

*This book is dedicated to beautiful,
magical YOU! May you always find
new and exciting ways to love yourself.
—M.R.R.*

Copyright © 2020 by Mechal Renee Roe

Step into Reading, Random House, and the Random House colophon are registered trademarks of Penguin Random House LLC.

Visit us on the Web!
StepIntoReading.com
rhcbooks.com

Educators and librarians, for a variety of teaching tools, visit us at RHTeachersLibrarians.com

*Library of Congress Cataloging-in-Publication Data*
Name: Roe, Mechal Renee, author, illustrator.
Title: I love being me! / written and illustrated by Mechal Renee Roe.
Description: First edition. | New York : Random House Children's Books, [2020] |
Series: Step into reading. Level one. | Audience: Ages 3–5. |
Summary: Illustrations and rhyming text reveal all of the things girls love about themselves, from their nose, toes, and skin to their ability to spin, run, and cook.
Identifiers: LCCN 2020010725 (print) | LCCN 2020010726 (ebook)
ISBN 978-1-9848-9560-8 (paperback) | ISBN 978-1-9848-9561-5 (library binding) |
ISBN 978-1-9848-9562-2 (ebook)
Subjects: CYAC: Stories in rhyme. | Self-esteem—Fiction.
Classification: LCC PZ8.3.R6185 Ial 2020 (print) | LCC PZ8.3.R6185 (ebook) | DDC [E]—dc23

Printed in the United States of America

10 9 8 7 6 5

This book has been officially leveled by using the F&P Text Level Gradient™ Leveling System.

# I Love Being Me!

by Mechal Renee Roe

Random House 🏠 New York

# I love being me!

# I love my nose!

# I love my toes!

I love to spin!

# I love my brown skin!

# I love being me!

I love to smile!
I love to
run a mile!

I love to
wash my hair!

# I love going
# to the fair!

# I love being me!

I love my eyes!

I love a

big surprise!

I love to knit!

I love my
baseball mitt!

# I love being me!

# I love to dream!

# I love my

# soccer team!

I love birds!

# I love new words!

# I love being me!

I love to cook!

I love to
read a book!

# I love to write!

# I love to fly a kite!

# I love being me!

I love to
plant flowers!

I love April showers!

25

I love school!

I love swimming
in the pool!

I love being me!

I love bugs!

I love my

grandma's hugs!

# I love my socks!

I love my locs!

# What do you love about being you?